1.39

EVERYONE EATS™

PASTA

Jillian Powell

RSVP®

RAINTREE
STECK-VAUGHN
PUBLISHERS

The Steck-Vaughn Company

Austin, Texas

Titles in the series

BREAD EGGS FISH FRUIT MILK
PASTA POTATOES RICE

Published by Raintree Steck-Vaughn Publishers,
an imprint of Steck-Vaughn Company
Everyone Eats™ is a trademark of Steck-Vaughn Company

Library of Congress Cataloging-in-Publication Data
Powell, Jillian.
Pasta / Jillian Powell.
p.   cm.—(Everyone eats)
Includes bibliographical references and index.
Summary: Discusses the history of pasta and noodle dishes,
how they are prepared, and their nutritional value, and provides
recipes for chow mein and sweet rigatoni.
ISBN 0-8172-4760-2
1. Pasta products—Juvenile literature.
2. Cookery (Pasta)—Juvenile literature.
[1. Pasta products.]
I. Title. II. Series: Powell, Jillian. Everyone eats.
TX394.5.P68   1997
641.3'31—dc20   96-32829

Printed in Italy. Bound in the United States.
1 2 3 4 5 6 7 8 9 0 01 00 99 98 97

Picture acknowledgments

Allsport 10; Cephas 8, 20, 25; Chapel Studios 9 (top), 11 (top), 12, 13 (bottom),
14, 15 (both), 16, 17 (both), 19 (top), 21 (top), 22–3, 24 (both); Mary Evans
7 (both); Eye Ubiquitous 4, 9 (bottom), 18, 21 (bottom); Life File 13 (top),
19 (bottom); Pasta Information Service 5; Wayland Picture Library title page,
contents page, 6, 11 (bottom).

Contents

The Healthy Fast Food

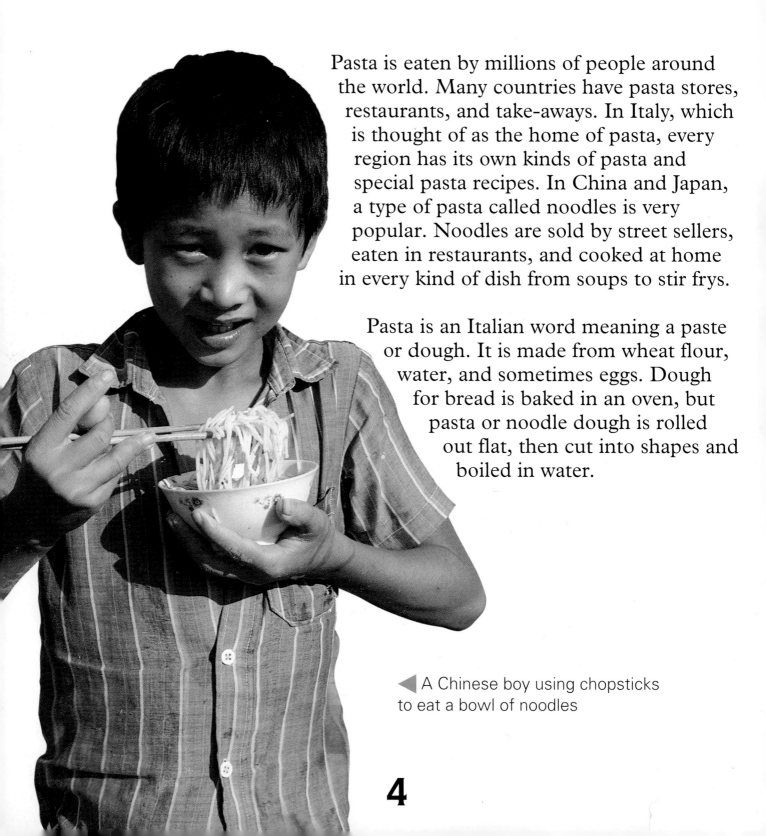

Pasta is eaten by millions of people around the world. Many countries have pasta stores, restaurants, and take-aways. In Italy, which is thought of as the home of pasta, every region has its own kinds of pasta and special pasta recipes. In China and Japan, a type of pasta called noodles is very popular. Noodles are sold by street sellers, eaten in restaurants, and cooked at home in every kind of dish from soups to stir frys.

Pasta is an Italian word meaning a paste or dough. It is made from wheat flour, water, and sometimes eggs. Dough for bread is baked in an oven, but pasta or noodle dough is rolled out flat, then cut into shapes and boiled in water.

◄ A Chinese boy using chopsticks to eat a bowl of noodles

Pasta comes in hundreds of different shapes, including ribbons, tubes, stars, shells, spirals, bows, and even cartoon characters and alphabet letters. Pasta can also be different colors.

Pasta is a fast food because it is quick and easy to cook. There are lots of ways to eat pasta: hot or cold, in soups, in salads, and with vegetable, meat, or sweet sauces.

Pasta is an energy-giving food that is good for you, especially if you eat it with healthy, low-fat foods like vegetable sauces and salads.

▲ Pasta is a healthy, energy-giving food and contains no additives (like artificial colors or flavors).

In Italy, the home of pasta, every person eats more than 50 pounds of pasta each year.

5

Pasta in the Past

People have been eating pasta for about 7,000 years. No one knows who invented pasta but we do know that it was eaten in ancient Egypt, China, and Japan and by the ancient Greeks and Romans. There are ancient wall paintings in Italy that show cooks making lasagne, and thin sticks found in Etruscan tombs may have been used for winding dough into macaroni. A recipe for strips of pasta fried with pepper and honey appears in one of the earliest recipe books, which was written by the Roman cook Apicius in the first century A.D.

▼ Freshly made Chinese noodles hanging up to dry in the sun. Noodles have been made like this in China for centuries.

Pasta was a popular food in the Middle Ages. Italian household accounts show that people bought macaroni and lasagne as well as special slotted spoons used for draining pasta. The thirteenth-century Italian explorer Marco Polo wrote that "Chinese noodles taste very good and similar to certain lasagne which we eat."

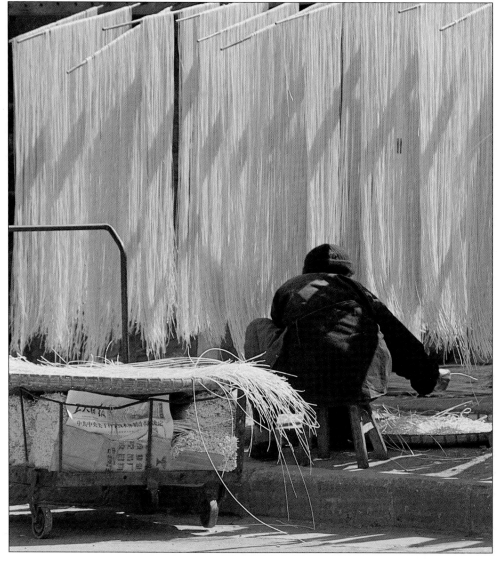

Pasta was made in factories during the nineteenth century in southern Italy, where the warm winds were ideal for drying the sheets of pasta. It was said that pasta makers knew more about the weather than sailors, because they knew exactly when the wind changed direction.

There is a story that the eleventh-century Saint Guglielmo was put in prison by his enemies and fed on ravioli (pasta pockets) filled with dry bran—but by a miracle, he changed the filling to cheese.

◀ An Italian pasta advertisement from 1940

Le migliori paste alimentari

▶ "Macaronis" were fashionable young men in eighteenth-century London.

The taste for pasta spread around the world. In 1789, Thomas Jefferson, who later became President of the United States, sent for a "machine for macaroni" from Naples, Italy. In Great Britain, during the eighteenth century, rich young men went on grand tours of Italy to study art and culture. This led to a fashion for everything Italian, including pasta. In London, there was a club whose members were called the "Macaronis" because they had fallen in love with Italy and pasta, especially macaroni. They even wrote poems in praise of pasta.

Pasta Today

Today, pasta can be bought in lots of different forms—fresh, dried, frozen, or canned. Most of the pasta we eat is made from durum wheat flour. Durum wheat produces a hard grain, which is ground into a rough yellow flour called semola. This is mixed with water and sometimes eggs to make pasta dough. The dough is rolled out into thin sheets and put into molds or cut into different shapes.

Fresh pasta is still made in many Italian homes. It can be made with a finely ground wheat flour called semolina or from buckwheat or wheat flour, like that used to make bread, mixed with eggs. Italian cooks are skilled at kneading and rolling the dough thin before cutting it with knives or putting it through hand-operated machines to make the different shapes.

▼ Pasta can be made into lots of different shapes by hand or by machine.

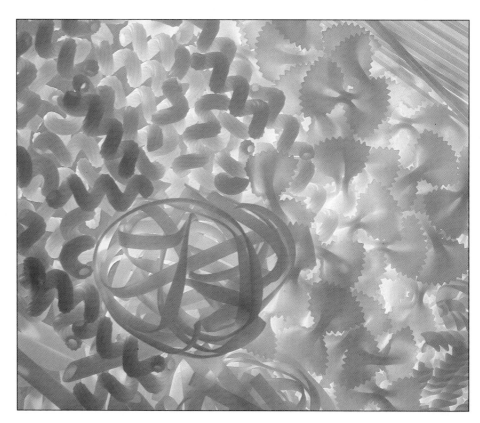

Fresh pasta can be bought in delicatessens and supermarkets as well as restaurants and take-outs. It takes only two or three minutes to cook in boiling water. It does not stay fresh and must be used in a day or two.

Most of the pasta we buy today has been dried, which means that it can be kept for several months. When it is cooked in boiling water the dry, hard shapes absorb water, soften and puff up. Dried pasta doubles in size and weight when it is cooked.

Noodles can be made from wheat or rice flour or ground mung beans. Sometimes egg is added to make egg noodles. Like pasta, noodles are also sold fresh or dried. Chinese noodle makers are very skilled and take four or five years to learn their craft. They knead, pull, toss, and twist the dough to make long, fine noodles. Dried noodles are soaked in water to soften them before cooking, and they take longer to cook than fresh noodles.

▲ Noodles can be many different sizes and colors.

▼ A skilled Chinese noodle maker at work

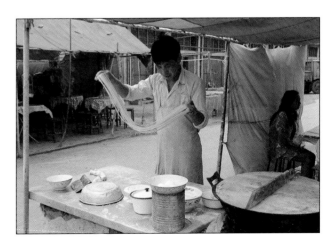

9

The Food in Pasta

Pasta is good for you. It contains lots of carbohydrates, which give you energy. Food energy is measured in calories. Other healthy foods such as bread, rice, and potatoes also contain lots of carbohydrates. High-carbohydrate foods are an important part of a healthy diet. Pasta is a filling food and contains half the calories of meat. Pasta is special because it releases energy more slowly than other foods.

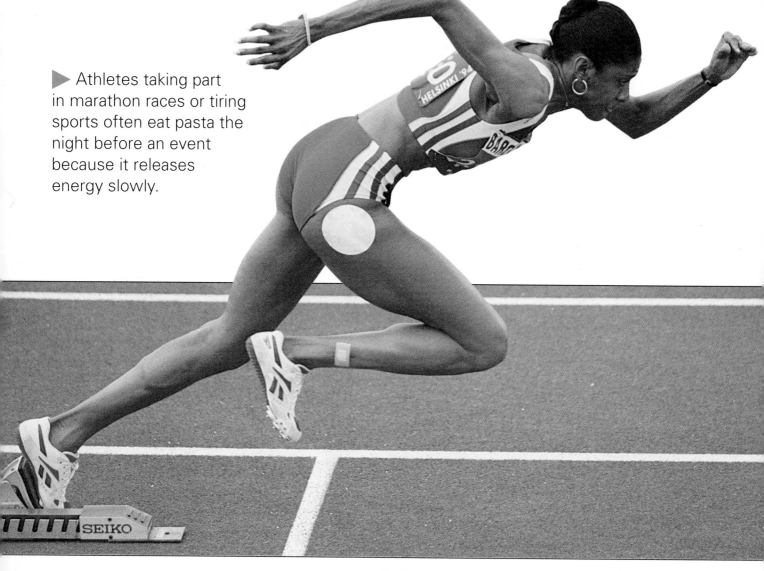

► Athletes taking part in marathon races or tiring sports often eat pasta the night before an event because it releases energy slowly.

2 ounces of dry wholewheat
spaghetti contains:

250 calories
47 grams of carbohydrate
11 grams of protein
3 grams of fat

◀ Wholewheat pasta (left) contains twice as much fiber as refined "white" pasta (right).

Pasta contains fiber, which is sometimes called roughage. Fiber helps us to digest food and pass it through our bodies. Wholewheat pasta is twice as good for you because it contains over twice as much fiber as pasta made with flour that has been milled to remove the bran.

Pasta contains protein, which is needed to build up the body and keep it healthy. Pasta has more protein than potatoes or rice and almost as much as beef, so it is good for vegetarians— people who choose not to eat meat. Pasta also gives us some of the vitamins and minerals that we need to help our bodies to work properly. For example, pasta contains the mineral iron, which keeps the blood healthy.

Pasta is low in fat, which is good because too much fat can damage the heart. It contains no added sugar or salt, which is good because sugar can harm the teeth, and too much salt is bad for the heart.

▲ Pasta is easy to cook and makes a filling and healthy meal.

11

A Pasta Factory

Pasta and noodles are made from wheat, the world's most widely grown cereal crop. The starchy grain is ground to make flour. At a pasta factory, the flour is mixed with water to make a paste. Eggs are added for egg noodles and for certain types of pasta like tagliatelle (see page 22) and for pasta that will be sold fresh, for cooking right away.

▼ Pasta is made from wheat flour ground from grains of wheat like these.

Pasta dough is pressed into molds or pushed through machines that cut out the different pasta shapes—strands, tubes, spirals, shells, and hundreds of other varieties. Some kinds of pasta, like ravioli and tortellini, are folded and filled with meat, cheese, or vegetables.

Pasta can be different colors because some ingredients add color. Wholewheat flour makes brown pasta, tomato or beet juice makes red pasta, and spinach juice makes green pasta.

Pasta numbers in tomato sauce is a popular children's dish, usually sold in cans.

Some factory-made pasta is made into ready-to-eat pasta dishes like macaroni cheese or spaghetti bolognese, which are chilled or frozen and just need to be re-heated. Dishes such as ravioli (meat-filled pasta parcels), spaghetti shapes in tomato sauce or minestrone can also be sold in tin cans, which keep fresh for a long time.

Pasta may also be dried, so that it will keep fresh in bags or boxes for several months. Pasta takes between forty and eighty hours to dry, depending on its shape.

Finally, the pasta is packaged and sent to stores to be sold.

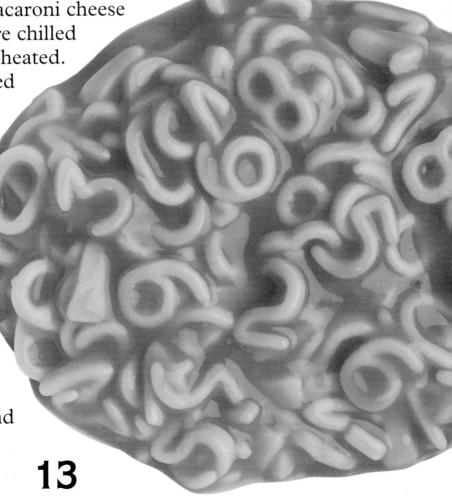

Making Pasta

Making pasta is very easy. Fresh pasta can be made in the kitchen at home with just a few simple ingredients.

To make fresh egg pasta, you will need:

1 medium egg
2/3 cup strong, unbleached plain flour

Carefully pour the flour into a pile on a big pastry board and use your hands to make a hole in the middle. Break the egg into the hole and use your hands to work the egg into the flour (this is called "kneading") until it sticks together and feels damp and stretchy. Don't let the dough dry out or it will be difficult to work with. If it starts to feel dry you can add a few drops of water. Now wrap the dough in a damp cloth and put it in the refrigerator.

◀ Kneading fresh pasta dough

After fifteen minutes, take out the ball of dough and use your hands to press it out into a circle on a floured board. Then use a rolling pin and, working from the middle outward, begin rolling out the dough. When you have a sheet of dough, turn it over, and roll it out again until it is thin and even.

Sprinkle it with flour, then leave it to dry for about thirty minutes before cutting out your pasta shapes. One way of making thin strips is to fold the sheet several times and then cut thin slices.

Your fresh egg pasta will take only two or three minutes to cook in boiling water.

▲ Using a rolling pin to make a thin, flat sheet of pasta. Dust the rolling pin with flour to keep it from sticking.

◀ Cutting out pasta shapes by hand

Cooking Pasta

Allow about 2 to 3 ounces of pasta for each person. You will need a large pan, about three-quarters full of water. Allow at least a quart of water for every 3 ounces of pasta.

Cover the pan and ask an adult to help you to put it on the stove and bring the water to a boil. Add a pinch of salt, then add the pasta and stir with a wooden spoon. Bring the water back to a boil, and then turn down the heat so that the water is bubbling fast but will not boil over.

▼ Pasta cooks quickly in boiling water.

If you are cooking fresh pasta, it will only take two or three minutes to cook. Dried pasta will take longer to cook—probably 9 or 10 minutes. You will find cooking times on the package.

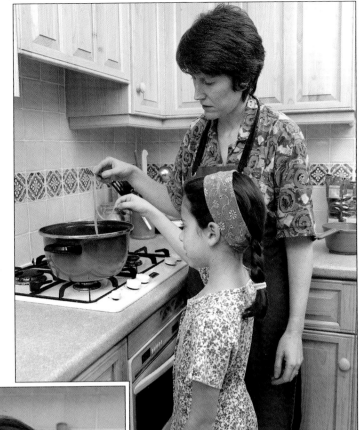

When you think the pasta is ready, ask an adult to remove a piece of pasta from the water. Let it cool slightly and then taste it to see if it is ready. Pasta should be slightly chewy—not too hard, but not too soft or mushy. The Italians call this cooking *al dente*, which means "to the tooth." You may have to let the pasta boil for a bit longer, then test it again.

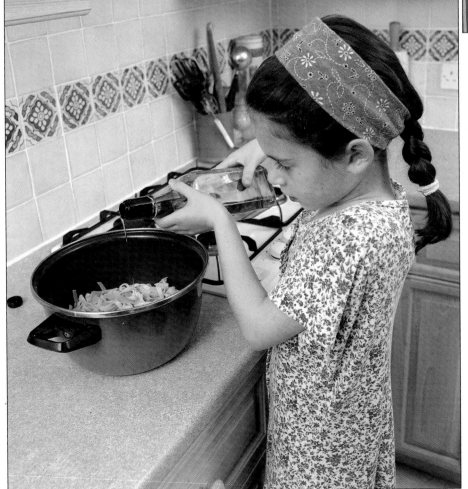

When your pasta is ready, ask an adult to help you take the pan off the heat and drain the pasta. You can stir in a few drops of olive oil or a little butter, which can help to prevent the pasta from sticking together.

Adding a little olive oil to cooked pasta

Italy—Home of Pasta

Italy is the home of pasta. Italians have been eating pasta for thousands of years, and every region has different kinds of pasta and many ways of cooking it. There are pasta stores that sell loose pasta, and many Italians still make fresh pasta at home. They eat it as an appetizer or main dish or dessert course, sometimes twice a day.

▼ Lasagne is a popular Italian dish of pasta, meat, vegetables, and sauce. It is eaten all over the world.

Special pasta dishes are eaten at Christmas time. Cappelletti ("little hats") are served at Christmas and New Year's, when they may be filled with left-over Christmas turkey. Passatelli is a pasta soup with cheese that is served in Bologna at Easter and during the spring. Pasta is also a popular holiday food. In Naples, baskets of hot pasta pies called pasticci and timballi are sold by street vendors on holidays.

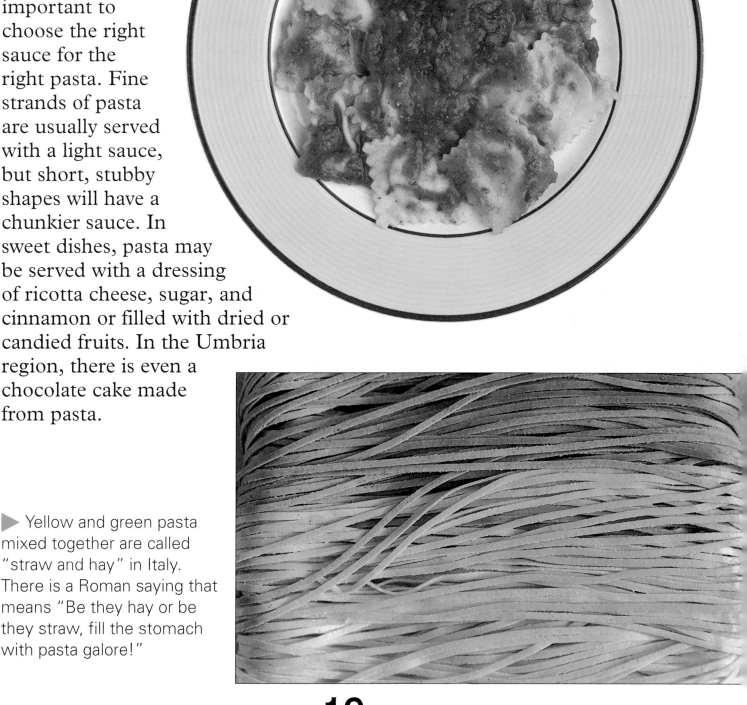

▶ Ravioli served with a tomato sauce

In Italy, it is important to choose the right sauce for the right pasta. Fine strands of pasta are usually served with a light sauce, but short, stubby shapes will have a chunkier sauce. In sweet dishes, pasta may be served with a dressing of ricotta cheese, sugar, and cinnamon or filled with dried or candied fruits. In the Umbria region, there is even a chocolate cake made from pasta.

▶ Yellow and green pasta mixed together are called "straw and hay" in Italy. There is a Roman saying that means "Be they hay or be they straw, fill the stomach with pasta galore!"

19

Italian Pasta Dishes

Pasta is eaten all over Italy, and different dishes are popular in each region of the country.

▲ Linguine—a favorite dish in the South

In parts of southern Italy, pasta is often served with seafood or hot sauces made with chili peppers.

Cooks in Abruzzi make a dish called *maccheroni alla chitarra*. The name comes from the machine used to make the pasta, which looks like a guitar. Egg pasta is rolled into flat sheets then pushed through wires on a wooden frame. It is served with hot chili sauce in locally made pottery bowls.

Cooks in Liguria add chopped herbs to their pasta dough. The pasta is served with pesto, a sauce made from basil, pine nuts, olive oil, and parmesan, a hard cheese.

Fettuccine, a type of noodle popular in Rome, is said to be the width of a dressmaker's tape and as straight as a Roman road. Also from Rome comes spaghetti carbonara, a dish that took its name from the charcoal burners in the woods who traditionally made this dish using spaghetti, bacon, eggs, and cheese.

Pasta is especially popular in Sicily. It was once said that every Sicilian dreamed of a Sicily made out of macaroni, with Mount Etna (a volcano in Sicily) as a mountain of grated cheese and the lighthouse in the harbor full of wine.

In Emilia Romagna, sweet pasta dishes are popular, including jam-filled ravioli and deep-fried tortelli filled with chestnuts and jam.

Minestrone is eaten all over Italy, although there are regional variations.

In Venice, thick soups made with pasta and beans are popular.

From Bologna comes spaghetti bolognese, which has a sauce made of ground beef, bacon, mushrooms, onions, tomatoes, and other chopped vegetables.

Turin

Milan

Verona

Padua

Venice

Genoa

LIGURIA

Bologna

EMILIA ROMAGNA

Florence

Spaghetti bolognese

Rome

ABRUZZI

In Naples, pasta was once sold in bags by street sellers. Today, pasta pies are often sold from baskets at festivals.

Naples

Bari

Tarranto

APULIA

In Apulia (called the "heel" of Italy) there is a special shape of pasta called orecchiette, which means "little ears" (see page 23). It is served with a tomato or seafood sauce.

CALABRIA

Palermo

Messina

SICILY

Catania

People from Calabria (called the "toe" of Italy) call pasta "ladies' curls" or "angel's hair." They serve it with sauces made from local foods like pine nuts gathered from the woods and spicy sausages.

An A to Z of Pasta Shapes

There are about 600 kinds of pasta, and new ones are being invented all the time. Pasta comes in flat sheets, like lasagne, tubes like macaroni and cannelloni, strings like spaghetti, and "nests" like vermicelli and tagliatelle. There are also spirals, shells, rings, and bows.

In Italy, each region makes its own traditional shapes, and they all have nicknames. For example, tortellini are known as the belly button of Venus, the Roman goddess of love. Italian cooks know which sauces to use with each kind of pasta.

Tagliatelle was said to have been created in 1487 in honor of the long hair of Lucrezia Borgia, a famous Italian noblewoman of the time. For centuries, Italian cooks argued over how wide tagliatelle should be. In 1972 it was decided that tagliatelle should be 8 mm (0.32 inches) wide when cooked; anything else was not tagliatelle.

1.
5.
2.
6.
7.
3.
8.
4.
9.

▶ A selection of various pasta shapes

Key

1. Elbow rigatoni	9. Farfalle
2. Fusilli	10. Gemelli
3. Cannelloni	11. Pappardelle
4. Conchiglie rigate	12. Lumache
5. Spaghetti	13. Rigatoni
6. Cappelletti	14. Penne
7. Orecchiette	15. Lasagne
8. Tagliatelle	16. Conchiglie

anelli	rings
bucatini	long tubes
cannelloni	large tubes
cappelletti	"little hats"
conchiglie	shells
farfalle	bows or butterflies
fettuccine	narrow ribbons
fusilli	corkscrews
gemelli	twins—two strands twisted together
lasagne	flat sheets
lumache	large "snails"
macaroni	short tubes
orecchiette	"little ears"
pappardelle	nests of wide strips
penne	pens (because they look like old-fashioned quill pens)
ravioli	stuffed squares
riccie	curly noodles
rigatoni	ridged tubes
spaghetti	strings
stelline	"little stars"
tagliatelle	nests of strands
tortellini	round twists of stuffed pasta
tortiglioni	twists
vermicelli	"little worms"
ziti	long macaroni

23

Pasta Dishes from Around the World

Pasta is eaten in many different ways around the world. In parts of Germany and eastern France, cooks make a special pasta called spätzle from flour, eggs, and cream. The fine strands are poached in boiling water then served with meat or cheese sauce.

▶ Creamy German spätzle, served with cheese sauce

▼ A Chinese dish of noodles and vegetables

Sometimes pasta is filled or stuffed, in dishes such as Chinese won ton, Russian pelmeni, Tibetan molmo, and Jewish kreplachs.

In China, Japan, and other eastern countries, noodles are popular and are eaten at all times of day from breakfast to dinner. They are boiled and eaten in soups and sauces, fried and served with meat and vegetables, or eaten cold in salads.

Noodles come in all shapes and sizes (see page 9). Flat noodles are usually used in soups and rounded noodles in stir-fry dishes. Noodles can be made from wheat or rice flour. Rice noodles are popular in southern China, where they are eaten with seafood. Bean thread or cellophane noodles are made from ground mung beans and are very fine strands that are almost transparent. Cooks deep fry them to serve with meat or vegetable dishes or put them in soups and casseroles.

▼ Noodles being cooked outdoors in a market stall in China

Egg noodles, which are made by adding egg to the pasta dough, are served with lots of different sauces, which can be made with fish, meat, chicken or vegetables. For a simple stir-fry, noodles may be fried with some bean sprouts and scallions in a little sesame oil, rice wine, and soy sauce.

Noodles are often served on birthdays in China and are traditionally eaten at New Year's, because the long strands represent long life. It is thought to be unlucky to cut them, as this might shorten your life.

25

Pasta Recipes for You to Try

Chow mein

For this stir-fry dish, a Chinese wok is best but you could use a large frying pan.

To serve four people you will need:

1/2 pound fresh or dried egg noodles

2 slices of bacon, chopped fine

1 tablespoon chopped scallions

2 ounces peas

1 teaspoon light soy sauce

1 tablespoon oil

1 chopped garlic clove

1/2 teaspoon sugar

1 teaspoon sesame oil

1 Cook the noodles, following the instructions on the package. Dried noodles will take a few minutes longer to cook than fresh noodles. Put the noodles in cold water to cool until you are ready to use them.

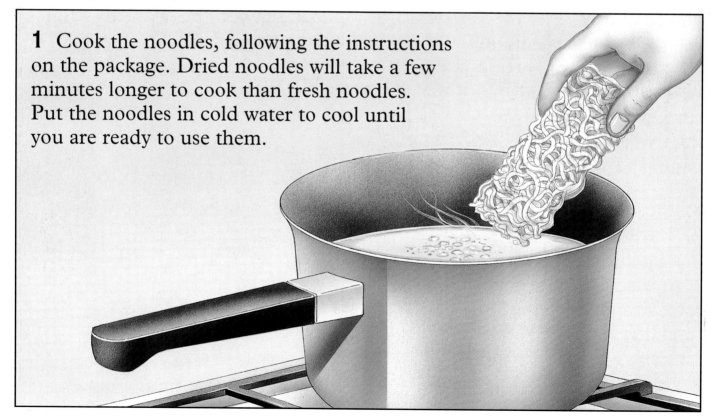

2 Ask an adult to help you to heat a tablespoon of oil in the wok or frying pan and fry the garlic for about ten seconds.

3 Add the peas and the bacon and keep stirring as you fry them for another minute.

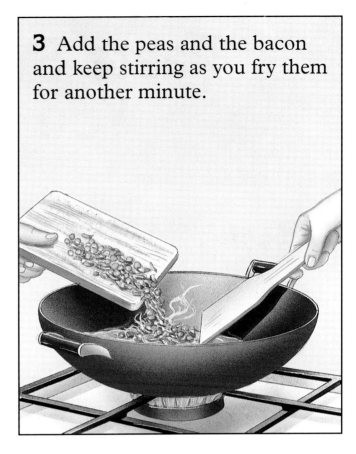

4 Drain the noodles in a sieve and put them into the pan with the soy sauce, sugar, and scallions. Cook, stirring well, for another two to four minutes.

5 Add the sesame oil, stir again, then put your chow mein onto a hot serving dish.

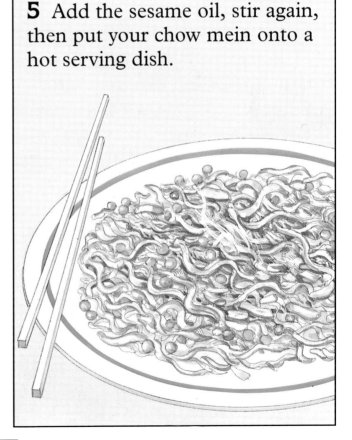

Sweet rigatoni

Try this sweet pasta as an unusual dessert.

To serve four people you will need:

1/2 pound of rigatoni or another short kind of pasta
4 ounces ricotta cheese
2 rounded teaspoons granulated sugar
1/4 teaspoon powdered cinnamon
about 1/3 to 1/2 cup milk

1 Ask an adult to help you heat a pan of water until it is boiling.

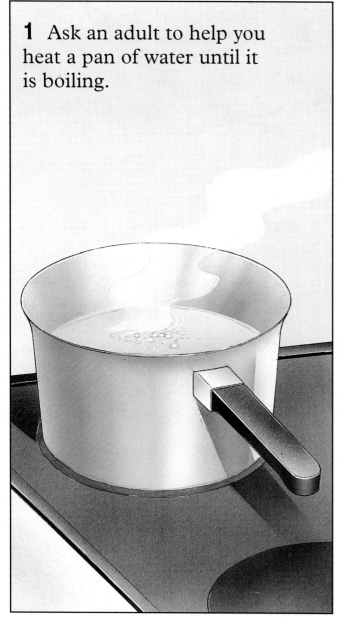

2 Add a pinch of salt to the boiling water, then carefully add the pasta. Stir with a wooden spoon and cook for the length of time stated on the package.

3 Pour the milk into a small saucepan and heat gently until it is just warm.

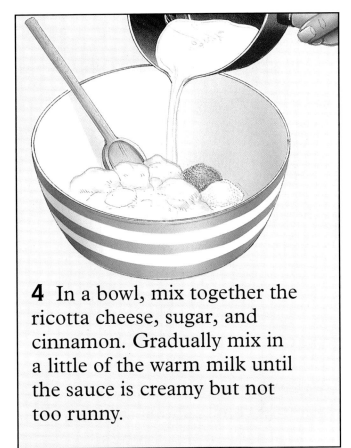

4 In a bowl, mix together the ricotta cheese, sugar, and cinnamon. Gradually mix in a little of the warm milk until the sauce is creamy but not too runny.

5 Ask an adult to help you to drain the cooked pasta, then mix it with the ricotta sauce and pour it into a warm serving dish.

Glossary

bran The coating of a cereal grain such as rice or wheat, between the outer hull and the inner seed.

calories Measurements of the energy in food.

carbohydrates Foods including sugars and starches, which give us energy.

cereal A kind of plant that produces grain.

charcoal burners People who burn wood very slowly, to make charcoal.

delicatessens Shops or parts of shops that sell fresh foods.

dough A paste of flour and water.

dressing A sauce that is put on food.

Etruscan Belonging to an ancient people who lived in central Italy before the Romans.

fiber A part of food that helps the body digest and pass food through.

grand tour A trip taken by rich eighteenth-century men to study the art and literature of Europe.

kneading Working and shaping with the hands.

marathon A long race.

Middle Ages The time in history from the sixth to the sixteenth century.

milled Ground up. Seeds and cereal grains are often milled.

minerals Substances, found in food, that we need to keep our bodies healthy.

mung bean A kind of bean grown in Asia.

poached Cooked in simmering liquid.

protein A substance, found in food, that we need to grow and repair our bodies.

roughage A substance, found in food, that helps our bodies to digest and pass food through.

starch A type of carbohydrate.

stir-fry A method of cooking by frying food quickly in oil, stirring it all the time.

vegetarians People who choose not to eat meat.

vitamins Substances, found in food, that we need to keep us healthy.

wholemeal and **wholewheat** The whole grain including the outer husk or bran.

wok A rounded Chinese pan used for frying food.

Books to Read

Food and Feasts series. New York: New Discovery. Historical glances at how various cultures ate the food they did and why these particular foods were eaten by the civilization.

Food Around the World series. New York: Thomson Learning. A series of ten books on food by country. Each book presents the particular ways in which the peoples of different countries prepare and serve their food. Simple recipes are also provided.

Dibble, Lisa. *Food and Farming.* New York: Dorling Kindersley, 1993.

Jones, Norma. *Food: What Do We Eat and Where Does It Come From.* Wylie, TX: Info Plus TX, 1992.

Kowtaluk, Hellen. *Discovering Food.* Peoria, IL: Bennet IL, 1982.

Moss, Miriam. *Eat Well.* New York: Macmillan Children's Group, 1993.

Perl, Lila. *Junk Food, Fast Food, Health Food: What America Eats and Why.* New York: Houghton Mifflin, 1980.

Tames, Richard. *Food: Feasts, Cooks, and Kitchens.* New York: Franklin Watts, 1994.

Index